The Bank of Dreams & Nightmares
20 Rax Lane, Bridport, DT6 3JJ

www.thebankofdreamsandnightmares.org

Published May 2022 by
The Bank of Dreams & Nightmares
Copyright © 2022 The Bank of Dreams & Nightmares

Creative Learning Manager / Editor
Janis Lane

Volunteer story mentors
Nick Goldsmith
Charlie Goldsmith
Alex Green
Eleanor James
Amberley Carter

Partner teacher
Naomi Gribler

Designer
Spike Golding

Illustrator
Yuhzen Cai

ISBN 978-1-7397340-0-8
Printed in Exeter by Imprint books
Distributed by The Bank of Dreams & Nightmares

I have a dream

Stories by writers from Beaminster School in Dorset

The Bank of Dreams & Nightmares encourages students to write pieces that are meaningful to them. In this vein, this publication contains pieces that address a range of issues, including some difficult topics. This book is intended for mature audiences, with topics, themes and language that may not be suitable for younger readers.

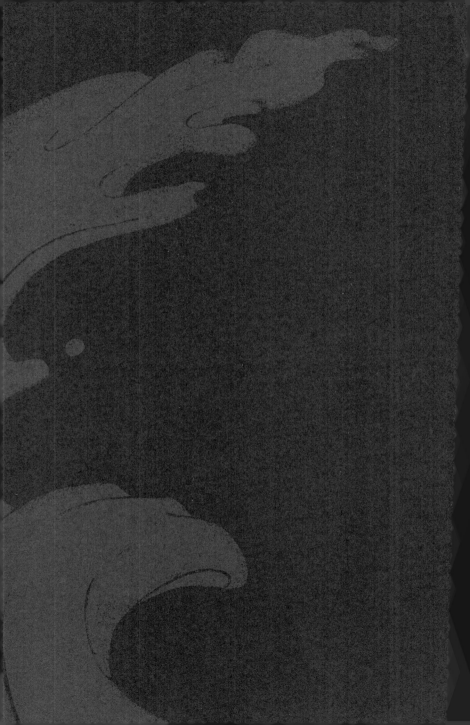

Contents

Foreword

I was driving through Beaminster recently and it was a normal busy weekday morning, people popping into shops, chatting on the street, going about their business. Little did I know that just up the road The Bank of Dreams and Nightmares was roaring, exploding, clattering into action in Beaminster School, firing up this extraordinary collection of stories. Pouring out of the school into the bright Dorset morning were these tales of betrayal, yearning, adventure, jeopardy, cold-blooded murder and chilling suspense.

These are not for the faint-hearted. These are stories of violence, death, terror and the uncanny. But they're also full of intelligent considerations of complex issues such as loyalty, identity and shifting states of consciousness. They contain fascinating insights into the emotional lives of teenagers living in strange times. It's very inspiring to me as a person who works with stories, to come across this work by young people which isn't afraid to engage with knotty subjects. This is what literature is for! For the moral, political, social and emotional grey areas, the tricky stuff. And it doesn't need to have answers, or make perfect sense, it can just be. It can shift and surprise. It can be very explicitly about the messed up world we live in, or it can re-design the world and examine it from a sideways place. These stories are laboratories where the writers have time and space to think. As one of the characters in one story says, writing is where they can "grow any idea".

Most exciting to me is that these stories are full of empathy. They try and see situations from more than one vantage point. They try and bridge the gap between souls, asking what it feels like to be lonely, or scared, or suddenly confronted with Gordon Ramsay.

Many of these stories deal with the pain and loneliness of being misunderstood, which can feel like being trapped. What is miraculous about creative writing, inventing, storytelling, is that we can write ourselves out of the trap, into other places, other planets, other skins. We can experiment, and play, and our ideas are free to roam.

It's a joy to think of these young people sharing their stories with each other, and wandering around their lives with stories buzzing about their brains. Nobody can police or own their imaginations, and the Bank of Dreams and Nightmares will always be open to them. It's a wonderful thing.

Max Porter
January 2022

I like Ya cut Je: The Holy Sus-Je-Sus

by Harry

Jesus was wandering around the green field with only one thought: Why is everyone acting so suspicious around me? The question was never-ending, as if he was actually sus! Jesus kept walking, until he saw an unusually tall cross. It was surrounded by hot orange fire. He felt a book flat underneath him, it read 'The Holy Sus'. A voice heard in the distance, "There is one Imposter among us."

Jesus woke up in a red spacesuit. He had a yellow note marked as 'Note 2 Self'. He attempted to take it off himself, but it was impossible. Jesus read the note in the mirror. "DUM"

"Help!" Jesus called. No one came to help. Jesus was scared; he had found a vent to hide in.

Jesus heard a loud beep. He was forced out of his vent! How? He was teleported to a messy room, it looked like a cafeteria. Jesus was accompanied by 14 other spacemen, each wearing space suits of different colours.

"I saw a dead body above MedBay via Security," Purple claimed.

Jesus was too worried to reply.

"I saw Pink dead on Vitals," Tan said.

"Are you the scientist? Blue asked, "Vitals isn't on this ship!"

"I saw Red in MedBay via admin," said Grey, "He seems pretty sus."

Soon after everyone started voting Jesus.

The results were in, and Jesus was ejected from the ship. What was the meaning of this? I like ya cut Je," he heard a voice in the distance say, "Je-sus!"

Jesus found himself nailed to a cross.

"What is the meaning of life?" Jesus asked out loud.

Then the crewmates lived a happily...

"No!"

"Rose was killed!"

"Call the meeting, now!"

Chapter 2: Juda-sus

Judas woke in a banana-coloured space suit. He felt a banana peel lying on his head. He tried to pull it off, but he couldn't.

"God, help me!" Judas said. No one came to help. Judas then heard what sounded like a backwards theme song.

"Haaiiil Satan!"

"Hehehehe."

"Line them up!"

"Grab your happy bag!"

"Yeeah, we're eating poop!"

"Doo-doo-doo-doo doo Dora!"

Meanwhile, a meeting was going on in another room.

"Rose's body was in MedBay," Yellow said.

"I don't know, but there was a suspicious sound coming from around there", Green said.

"Wait, where did Brown go!?", Purple asked.

Soon after, the meeting ended, and no one had voted.

Judas looked around and he saw a dead body It was coloured Rose. Judas was terrified, he looked behind himself. It was a brown dead body! It had a toilet roll on top of it. Judas heard the same echoing voice.

"Yeeah, we're all eating poop!"

"Line them up!"

Judas saw a ghost; it was pink coloured!

"AAAH! GOD, PLEASE COME, HELP ME!" Judas cried.

Judas ran away.

"Imposta, imposta!" a White crewmate said.

"Hand it in! Banana, Imposta, remember your imposta!"

Judas stopped.

"What is imposta?"

"Give me your MIRA card, pay your imposta."

"What is a…?"

"DEAD BODY REPORTED!"

"Trust me, it's Banana," White said, "He won't pay imposta."

"Only Impostas don't have MIRA cards," Black said.

"Yes, that's right, Banana is the Imposter," White said.

The results were in, everyone voted Judas.

Judas woke up floating in space.

"Judas was not the Imposter!"

"No!" "Our life, it's ended!"

Judas saw the remaining crewmates die before his eyes.

THE BAD ENDING

"Doo-doo-doo-doo doo Dora!"

"Line them up!"

"Hehehehe"…

"Bye, JUDA-SUS!"

"Hola, say Dora!"

Dora the Explorer theme starts playing

The adventure continues in 'Dora the Explorer!'

Note: This story is a prequel to 'Dora the Explorer (a children's TV show)

Why Me?

by Callum Harmer

Chapter 1 - Jack

As I stare at the bottom of my empty cup in my cold hands, my mum is talking to a doctor; she turns and looks at me. She thanks the doctor and walks over to me and puts her hand on my shoulder.

"Come on then let's go home."

Chapter 2 - Tia

"I just want you to know that this doesn't make you any less smarter than you are."

"I know mum," Jack said, emotionless.

"The doctor said Jack's got dyslexia. Did you hear? Our son has dyslexia. I'm trying to not make this get him down. He's a smart boy I know that, but he does struggle sometimes."

Chapter 3 – Jack

My dad is dead.

I've got dyslexia.

Why me?

I wanna be normal.

"Jack, dinner's ready."

"Shut up and bring it here then."

"Alright, coming."

"Hurry up and leave it outside."

Chapter 4 – Tia

Jack can be rude sometimes, but I let him at a time like this. As I carry his dinner up to his room I slip on his school bag and the food goes everywhere.

Chapter 5 – Jack

"Mum, how could you, you idiot? Clean it up while I go on a walk."

As I walk out of the door I hear mum talking to herself.

Chapter 6 – Tia

Jack's pushed it now; he should have helped me tidy this up. I'm picking up the meatballs as I'm hoping Jack is safe…

Chapter 7 – Jack

The cold air hitting the back of my neck, the feeling of being followed came over me.

I turn around.

Nothing was there.

A noise.

I turn around again.

A suspicious looking van slowly goes past and pulls over.

My mind wants me to run but my legs won't move.

Chapter 8 – Ross

They think I'm dead.

I only left for their own safety. I didn't want to see them get hurt.

Chapter 9 – Jack

I've got a feeling a bad thing is gonna happen; the van doors start to creak open.

"Dad?"

The 'Boy' on the Bridge

by Jay Mullany

The wind blows through my hair. This is it.

Tears roll down my face, silent sobs in between each cry. Nobody will see me for who I am, for who I aspire to be.

I step forward and close my eyes.

"Goodbye," I whisper, my raspy voice getting caught in my throat.

"Wait!" he screams, sounding desperate.

Michael is 15, two years older than me and he is a hottie. His eyes are hazel brown, his hair maroon coloured. I imagine he's got a six-pack, but I've never seen his arms or chest. Nobody has.

He sits in front of me in maths, though I never thought he'd acknowledged me.

I recognise that scream; I knew it was Michael.

He runs up to me, despite the traffic, and holds me tight. His breath is raspy and warm which gives me butterflies. He cares. He actually cares about me.

We stand there, frozen in shock. Out heartbeats align and beat in sync as we stand clutching each other. He must think I'm stupid. Why did he save me? Why couldn't I just jump?

I start uncontrollably sobbing into his arms. He winces but holds on to me tight. We walk off the bridge and back to his. I'm exhausted so I collapse onto his bed, my eyes blurry. My life blurry.

"Why were you up there, Charlie?" he whispers, holding me tight.

"Charlotte, actually," I say, a scared look on my face. He looks at me, smiles and then cuddles me from behind.

"Well, Charlotte, I care about you. I see you. I'm here," he exclaims.

"People may not seem like they care but they do. They really do," he adds.

Michael takes his shirt off and hops into bed. It's dark outside and late. I get shocked when I see all the bruises on his chest and the cuts scattered on his arms. Why is he so injured? What happened?

His parents aren't home, which is good.

"Do they abuse you?" I cry.

He doesn't say anything. But he nods. The popular boy doesn't have the perfect life whatsoever.

We lay there in silence, the night among us. Now we both know the truth about each other. Now the truth's out, we don't need to hide any more. We have each other. The truth is, he saved me. If I died, nobody would see me for who I am; now they do. Now they all know.

My name is Charlotte Glover, and I am transgender.

My Dream

by Katie

Chapter 1 – My Monday Morning

Hi. My name is Izzy and I'm 15 years old and my dream is to sing at the biggest concert in America, but my mum is very sick and I'm the only one who can take care of her.

"Morning mum, I made breakfast."

"Thank you but I'm not really hungry."

"Are you sure you'll be okay while I'm at school?"

"I'll be fine."

I'm off to school thinking about what I want to do when I leave here. I'm daydreaming when I bump into James. Big James.

Big James is 15 years old. Everyone is scared of him apart from his friends. Of course, I'm late and have to bump into Big James – my Monday morning is definitely not going well.

"Oi, you get back here," James shouts.

"Please, I'm late to class," I say quietly.

"Does it look like my face cares?"

"I have to go, I'm sorry,"

"Right, meet me here at the end of the day."

"I can't."

"Why?"

"My mum is sick. She needs me.

"LIAR!" James shouts, angrily.

"Right, I'm leaving."

Chapter 2 – The Dreaded Phone Call

I'm on the way to class and my phone is ringing. It's mum.
A shiver runs down my spine.

"Hi mum, are you ok?"

"Yes sweetheart, can you grab some milk?"

"Yes of course, you scared me."

"Well, I'm ok. See you later."

It's finally the end of the day, there's a cake sale and I was going
to buy one but now I have to buy some milk. The smell of sweet,
wonderful cupcakes is making me so hungry. I'm staring into space
dreaming about the huge stage in America with a microphone
as big as my head. The crowd is cheering and I'm singing my
heart out having the time of my life. The sun is shining. Then my
daydream ends and I'm back in the playground. I jump out of my

skin and James is right next to me.

"Hello Izzy, are you ok?"

"Oh, I'm okay, please I don't have time for you."

"Ok, chill."

I'm on my way home buying milk from the shop, when I get a phone call from a private number – the most dreaded phone call I have ever received.

"Hi, who is this?"

"Hi, this is the doctor.

Oh, no.

"I'm afraid your mother has passed away."

I arrive home. My heart has sunk, and I feel lost. The house is empty. The smell of mum's oxygen mask is making me think of her. A broken glass of water scattered along the kitchen floor. Guilt travels over me and I think to myself; *if I hadn't gone to school my mum would still be alive.* I go over to the sofa and bury my head in a pillow, I scream and cry with guilt, anger, and sadness.

There's a knock at the door and it's James. I get butterflies in my stomach. I think I like him. I think to myself, *No I can't, he is horrible.*

"What are you doing here?" I said.

"I'm sorry that I've been horrible to you; I didn't know what you were going through."

"Thank you for being sorry."

Chapter 3 – My Dream Comes True

Five years later...

I'm now 20 years old and my mum has been dead for five years, and I miss her so much. Big James was caught five years ago being horrible to me and ever since he's been so nice, and I can't stop thinking about him; he's always texting me.

I have an audition tomorrow that could change my life.

It's finally the day. The man gives me a song. I'm singing in front of him and it's going amazingly...

It's the end of the audition. I've got my fingers crossed. I'm terrified but excited as well.

"Izzy, you made it – you will sing on Christmas Eve."

"Oh my, thank you."

* * *

It's finally Christmas Eve; butterflies feel in my stomach. I get a vision of my mum. Clear as day.

"Hey sweetie, you'll do great. I miss you."

"I miss you too."

I try to touch her, but she vanishes.

I walk out onto stage. Thousands of people staring at me. The spotlight hovers over me. The music plays and I sing; it's amazing.

I can see James and I think, *I want to be with him*. Every time I see him I get butterflies.

* * *

It's the end of the show. James comes over to me.

"Izzy, I'm so proud of you."

"It was the most amazing dream."

"Your mum would be proud."

He leans in close for a kiss. Butterflies fill my stomach.

This is my childhood dream.

The Story of Ellie Comb

by Ellie-May Pearce

Chapter 1

I have a name, which is Ellie Comb, but my friends call me Elle. I heard a knock at the door and it was my sister (ugh I love, hate her); her name is Hayley not that it is important. Although I'm ready to go to school my best friend comes and picks me up - her name is Zoe, we are both in Year 11. As we walk to school my sister always says mean stuff, but Zoe tells her to shut it - LOL.

Mr Evenbrouer was getting us at school but told Zoe to take out her nose and lip thing. They end up fighting over it but as I turned I saw a good-looking guy.

I said "OMG." Zoe and Mr Evenbrouer turned and looked surprised! Mr Evenbrouer shouted, "Woah, woah, woah, No, get off NOW!"

They were travellers and one said, "Please, we need to camp

somewhere because the mayor has kicked us off our land."

Mr Evenbrouer wanted to say, "No, just take yourselves somewhere else, you're not staying, goodbye."

I quickly shouted "no, um."

Zoe came in and saved me: "They have as much right to be here as I have, we all come from different places, Sir."

Mr Evenbrouer replied, "Not now Zoe, I know you're a different colour, but this is different."

One traveller got out of his car and yelled, "Oi, is that racism Sir?"

Then Mr Evenbrouer did nothing but a few minutes later he slowly said, "Fine, you can stay on the school field."

Soon, after a few minutes, we all went inside including a boy and a girl that just walked past us, but the girls walked on while the boy stopped.

He whispered, "Thanks, but don't help next time. Oh by the way, I'm Marcus."

Then Marcus ran after that girl.

Zoe quickly answered to me, "What did he want?"

I replied, "Oh nothing, he just wanted to say thanks to us all."

Then I walked off as the bell went for first lesson, which was cooking. I hated that teacher – she's so strict. Marcus was sat next to my chair. The teacher said, "Good morning class. Today we are cooking so I'm pairing you up. So, Marcus and Ellie, Zoe and Lucy, and then everyone else can pair up."

As I walked over to my cooking desk Marcus was already there. I quickly walked over to him.

I said, "Hi Marcus."

He whispered, "Hello, what's your last name, I never got it."

I whispered back, "Oh um Comb, Ellie Comb."

Then the teacher started to explain what we were doing today.

Forty-five minutes later, after we had baked muffins, it was second lesson, but it was my free period. Then as I walked out of the class, I had forgotten my books. So, Marcus ran after me. Catching his breath, he said, "Hi again, you forgot your books."

I replied, "Oh hi. Thanks."

Zoe started to walk over. She said, "Hi Marcus, you liking it here? Oh, hey Elle."

She rolled her eyes at me. Marcus replied grumbly, saying, "Well I'm sorry Zoe, but I thought Ellie was your best friend. Anyway, it's nice here, better go - see you later Comb, Ellie Comb."

I quickly shouted "Bye, wait, hey."

Then Zoe and turned and yelled, "Haha do you think he would ever go out with you, you're so ugly. I was pretending to be your friend to get friends with your sister."

As she yelled that, I was getting sad and started to cry. I sprinted to the bathroom and hid in the stall for the rest of the day. At the end of the day Hayley ran to me and shouted saying, "Hey I'm so sorry I had no idea! Please believe me."

I didn't reply all the way home.

"Pleeeeeeeeeeeeeeeeeeaszzzzze."

The buzzing of my alarm woke me up.

I whispered, "Oh phew, it was just a dream."

Chapter 2

I quickly got changed and ready for school. My mum called me and Hayley down for breakfast. The stairs carpet was so hard it hurt my feet. Once I was downstairs Hayley said, "Hey sis, ready for school?"

I replied, "Yeah I am, thanks."

Mum had cooked bacon and eggs for us; she said, "Dig in."

Hayley and I both yelled, "Thanks mum, is Mr Evenbrouer still here?"

Mr Evenbrouer and our mum were together in a relationship! Mum didn't reply to us. Mr Evenbrouer was coming downstairs after having a shower.

"Good morning girls. Come on, we'd better get to school. I'll drive."

Once we were in the car ready, mum and Mr Evenbrouer were kissing goodbye. We were at the school gate after a 20-minute drive. I saw Zoe. Mr Evenbrouer parked the car and ran to her and asked for her lip and nose thing. Zoe and Mr Evenbrouer were fighting. I turned and shouted.

"OMG."

They both turned, looking surprised.

There were travellers on the school grounds. There was one on a horse without a helmet. Mr Evenbrouer shouted, "Woah, no, stop, not here. You don't…nope, just no."

I shouted, "No, um."

Zoe jumped in and saved me. She yelled, "They have as much right to be here as I have, sir."

Mr Evenbrouer yelled back, "Not now, Zoe. You know what, you can have the school travellers but on one condition: that the boy on the horse and the girl next to him come to school."

So, the boy got off the horse and walked past.

The boy stopped and whispered, "Thanks, but don't help next time. Oh, by the way, I'm Marcus."

Carnage*

By Ben Hoare (y9)

There was blood and it didn't stop.

There was screaming.

There was screaming and blood.

There were growls and death. There were dead people walking. The dead people were stumbling across the place. They took them away.

"I was left alone in the dark. They left me to die."

"George! Come here! Did you find it?"

George whistled me over. I shot my arrow for the nose of the deer; it fell down to the ground. I dragged it back to the quadbike with guilt and wedged it onto the trailer and rode home. I opened the deceased deer with tears rolling down my cheek.

He lives in a tower block in east London where the air smells fresh but also stale.

The air smells fresh from the plants but also smells stale from the dead people walking.

The dead, man-eating people walking.

The Nightmare

by George S.

Chapter 1 – The Beginning of the Nightmare

I want to go to sleep. I've had restless nights and endless nightmares. I wonder what will happen if I go to sleep tonight? It is Friday the 13th, after all.

Chapter 2 – The Massacre

I woke up to a blood curdling scream. I instantly ran upstairs. I opened the door to the living room, and I suddenly stopped in my tracks. What I saw was horrifying: my whole family had been ripped in half. Some had sword marks in their heads. I felt absolutely devastated that someone would massacre my family. Who would do such a thing?

Chapter 3 – …

After what I witnessed, I ran back downstairs. I put on my shoes and ran outside into the dark, damp streets. I kept running and running but couldn't get to the end of the street! Then I thought to myself, *Am I in a nightmare?* No, I couldn't be in a nightmare! Is it just me or is this street stretching out before my eyes?

I looked down at the street and saw a blood trail leading to a shack in the road. There were no cars and no other people. The street looked abandoned …but it can't be! It's never looked abandoned before, so why now?...

Chapter 4 – The Shack

When I approached the shack, it looked abandoned. There were cobwebs, ivy, and moss growing all over it. I'd never seen this shack before! Why is it here in the first place? Anyway, let's not worry about that now, let's go inside…

Chapter 5 – This is the End

As I stepped inside, I saw nobody in the shack. There was no furniture, just cobwebs, ivy, and moss. There were no windows, but I could've sworn I'd seen them outside. It's almost as if the shack was bigger on the inside. Suddenly, the door shut behind. I started frantically pounding on the door, begging for someone to help… but nobody came!

Chapter 6 – The Thing

I slowly turned around. Then I saw it. The thing that killed my parents. It was an exact replica of me!

"What are you?!" I asked.

It answered, "I am the God of this realm, I created this universe so that you can endlessly suffer."

"Why would you kill my family?" I asked. "Why? Why? Why?!!!"

I pounced on it! I punched it, I kicked it. It felt no pain.

Then it attacked me. It copied me. It knew my every move. I couldn't kill it. We fought over the realm that the replica had created.

The nightmare began to crumble; it started to fall apart. Behind the nightmare was an endless void of nothing, except darkness.

I had finally killed it.

How do I escape this nightmare now?! This nothingness, this void. Am I here forever…?

THE END?

We're All Mad Here. Aren't you?

By Buster

I have a dream to meet a man with power.

Hi, my name is Max, I'm in year 8 and it is my first day in this year. I was nervous but when I was walking down to school I heard a voice calling my name. I turned to my right and I saw an old man with grey eyes and grey hair, and he said, "You look worthy enough, have these."

He gave me a pack of Tarot cards. I was going to ask why he gave them to me, but he vanished. I was thinking what to do with them, but I looked at my watch and I saw the time: 9am. I was going to be late, so I started to sprint all the way to school, and I made it just in time. I was breathing heavily, and my legs were in pain but I made it so that was all that mattered. I was walking down to the hall and two-year 11s walked up to me.

"Hey kid how old are you?"

"I'm 12."

"You don't look 12, you are probably 9 judging by your size"

"Hey!"

"Anyways, give us your money."

"I have no money."

"Well then give us your bag."

"No! I refuse."

"Well then, I hope you like sleeping."

All of a sudden time stopped and the Tarot cards were glowing. I was hesitant, but I pulled one out, and the card said DEATH. Suddenly the two boys slammed to the ground, lifeless. *What happened, did I do this? But how?* I was frozen with thoughts and a teacher came by:

"What happened here, why are those boys on the ground?"

The teacher flipped the boys over and saw they were lifeless; the teacher screamed with fear and ran off and called the police. I didn't know what to do, but the police showed up...

"Freeze, put your hands up now"

So, I did what they said. They took me in their car and put me in their interrogation room.

"What did you do to them?"

"I don't know," I replied. "All I did was pull a Tarot card and they died."

The police were frozen for a minute.

"What did you say, Tarot cards? What card was it?"

"Death"

"Death, you say?"

How did that make sense? the police thought.

"Hey kid, pull Death again."

"OK."

So, I did it, but.... Nothing happened.

"See nothing happened"

"Well kid you still have to go court"

"Court!" I shouted, "I'm only 12 years old how can you take me to court?"

"Sorry kid, but you are nearest to the bodies, so you have to go to court, rules are rules, he replied.

I was getting nervous, very nervous, I didn't know what to do so I just had to wait. What a day. The next day happened, and I had to go to court.

"Order, order, we are here to trial Max. What do you have to say Max?"

"I'm innocent," I say. "Believe me, please."

"Can the witness speak?"

The teacher came out.

"I saw him just standing there, and the two boys were lying dead on the ground, he had to have done it. Who do you trust more your honour, the boy or me?"

"Well since he is a kid, I have to believe you m'am."

"No, I am innocent, believe me please I am begging."

Wait, no, no I can't go to prison yet, I thought. The judge was about to say something, but the tarot cards begun to glow again. In desperation I pulled one out and it said, The Hanged Man.

Suddenly the judge said:

"Not Guilty."

Everyone was in shock. In my head I thought *I am free, and I am now liberated*; I walked out the courthouse with a grin.

It has been two days since the incident at the courthouse. I was trying to think what the Tarot cards are and why did I get them, and why do I have this power. But when I was thinking, my mum said something from downstairs.

"Dinner's ready Max."

"Coming," I replied.

I love my mum's cooking, she is the best in the world. Today I had roast potatoes, lamb, carrots, some turkey covered in gravy. It was all amazing, the smell, the taste, it was like heaven for me.

Gone

by Logan (Juan)

"What…where have all the adults gone?" Edillio said to his twin Juan, sat in maths class.

The teacher Ms Carson has just disappeared right in front of their eyes. Everyone sat in silence until all of a sudden, fire bells rang and made the twins' ears throb loudly. They sprinted out to their house and checked everywhere…no one answered their cries. She was gone too. Their new mission was to find their mum.

They started walking all around town and walked into many people who were on a journey to find the people who looked after them. They found many teenagers gathering at the town centre, one of the kids from the rival school trying to take over.

Juan and Edillio jumped up onto the stage and pushed him off to get the crowd's attention. They demanded everyone listened to them. The questions they hoped people knew the answer to, were asked.

"Where are the adults?"

No one answered. The awkward silence made them angry; they

both ran off stage to the park where their mum used to take them every Tuesday. The dark, quiet night made them go crazy. Juan started pounding things because he had failed. Edillio was reassuring himself that they would definitely find their mum.

"Are you ok bro?" Edillio said to his brother, who was sat down on the swings looking emotionless.

"Yeah, just thinking," Juan said.

"'Bout what?" Edillio whispered.

"Well, if all the adults have disappeared does that mean we will go away in three weeks, on our 18th?"

"Hopefully. I miss mum."

They both knew someone had to step up and take care of the children in the nursery. They had to…but would they? They both walked over to the anxious and afraid young kids to reassure them everything would be fine and they would find their mums and dads. They all stopped talking and thanked the twins. They felt proud and happy that they could reassure people things would be alright. An idea hit them: what if they became the 'major' to help everybody with all of their problems?

So, they both went back to the very stage where they had just been, but with a different mindset. They caught everyone's eye and stared into the crowd and started talking to the children about hope, what was going to happen, and how good this was.

Three weeks later everything was fine but with just one day before their 18th birthday everyone was paranoid that the two people who had earned everyone's trust were going to disappear.

They had a party and a very early night; both woke up the next day in the same beds they slept in. They burst into tears until a familiar voice called for them both from downstairs.

"Wait, MUM!" They both screamed as loud as they could …

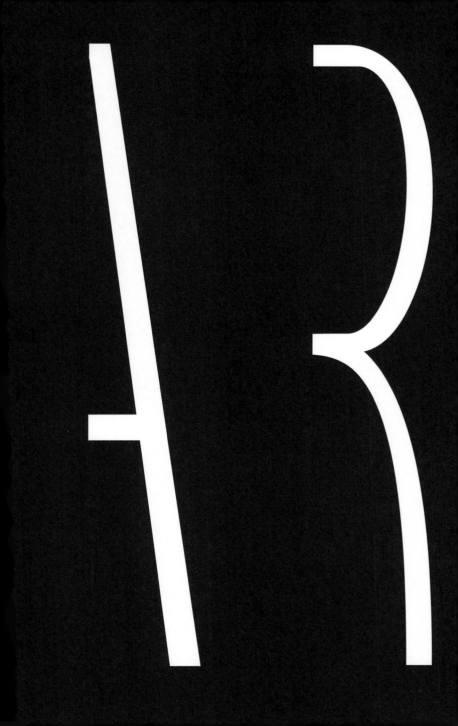

The Book

by Lola Kehoe

Part 1

I worked in the school library. I wanted a book I had not read yet.
For some odd reason one specific book stood out. I looked at the
cover and it was about crystals. I loved crystals. I have a special
one. It represents my birthday which is 19.7.2020. My special
crystal is called pearl and feels smooth and round and shiny, and
is pink. I am 11-and-a-half. I took the book because no one was
there. I did not know the power of this book. I walked out with the
book and went home. Before a hard thing hit the floor.

Meanwhile the librarian was working and found the book gone.
When she found the pearl I had dropped she knew it was me that
had taken the book.

At home I went straight to my room. I was desperate to read it.
I read the blurb and it said, 'An interesting way to get any magic
crystal you want but I must warn you if you open the book you
cannot close the power of it.'

I thought for a minute.

I opened the book and immediately everything lifted up. The air felt strange, and a cold chill went down my back. It smelt dusty and disgusting. It made it hard to breathe. What I saw was unbelievable and totally out of this world. I heard a whooshing sound as everything flew around. The air tasted magical as the book started to glow.

Part 2

The book opened. I wanted to touch the book, but I couldn't… my hand fell through it. I wanted to know what was inside but at the same time I was repelled. I stuck my head in the book and saw a load of colours. I wiggled further into the colours, but it all became BLACK…

"Arrr!"

I fell into nothing.

Bang. I hit the floor.

A dust cloud came up.

I stood up.

A light turned on…

Part 3

A stranger came out of nowhere.

He whispered, "Hi."

I said, "Hi."

He said, "Shut up whispering, someone is listening and if they found out I will, I will die."

"Ok," I whispered.

"Your paper, get it out."

"What paper? I don't have any."

"Look in your pocket," he said.

I looked in my pocket and found paper that said:

TASK 1

Find a pearl and return it to the mermaid at the bottom of the sea and return it to her crown.

TASK 2

Find the pearl half and activate the thing.

"I had the task when I was here."

"Oi, I am reading."

"Oh, sorry,' he said.

"Where first?"

"The sea."

At the sea we looked around trying to find the pearl on the map. I put it back in my pocket but found a map that lit up where the treasure is. It said it was high up in a bird's nest. I had to climb the tree to get it.

Back on the ground I had the pearl. I dove into the sea, but I could not hold my breath. I came to the surface and said, "I can't hold my breath."

He said, "You can breathe in the water," so I went under and gave the pearl to the mermaid.

I pulled out the paper and went to Task 2. I dug, trying to find the pearl, but I could not. I dug through the sand and found it.

We made it out but the man inside was in there for 25 years. After that I locked the book away.

25 Years Later…

My child went into the book.

Trapped*

by Evey (y9)

There was a black silhouette in the distance. It looked like it was a person, I couldn't tell who. As I got closer it looked like they had their phone in one hand but a knife in the other. Pacing. Up and down under the light. Nervously, I crept closer. Wondering what was going to happen next. It was eerie. I was a couple of steps away when the silhouette turned around. I couldn't really see who he was because he was wearing a big coat and a mask. As they turned around I asked them, "Are you ok?"

They looked at me and replied, "Yes I'm fine. Now leave." In a manly voice.

Who are they? I thought.

"Um, are you in trouble?" I wondered, worryingly.

"No, I'm not, someone will be here in a min_"

He paused. His phone rang. He took it out of his pocket and looked at it. Before he answered it he turned to me and said quickly, "I think you should leave."

*Title chosen by Editor
50

I went to turn around and quietly replied, "Okay, whatever you say."

Suddenly I felt an arm go around my neck and something cold touch the side of my head. I tried to move but he clenched onto my head tighter. I couldn't breathe. Again, I tried to move out of the headlock and being strangled, but I couldn't. Then his leg wrapped around mine and he threw me on the floor. I could breathe, but it hurt. I wasn't being held. I went to try to get up and he kicked me down to the floor again. A couple of minutes went past and no one had moved.

He was on his phone again, and he seemed distracted. I tried again to stand up and escape but again he kicked me down and held a gun to my head; I got shivers down my spine.

Five minutes later…

His phone rang again. This was my moment to either run or call the police. So, as he stood up, I discreetly got my phone out of my pocket and called 999. Luckily he answered his phone so that gave me ten minutes to whisper over the phone, to get help. Once I knew help was on the way I felt better, but I was still scared. The police were 25 minutes away, but he got off the phone and whispered, "Ten minutes, only ten minutes to survive."

I was shaking, scared, worried.

10 minutes later…

I heard a car coming up behind us. I opened my eyes; there were bright lights above my head. The bloke picked up three bin bags and chucked them in the car. Then, he walked over to me and stood over the top of me.

"Get up!" he shouted.

"What? Why?" I trembled.

"Don't ask questions. Just do it." He grabbed my arms and pulled me up, walked me over to the car, pushed me in and slammed the car door.

Who is the driver? I said to myself, worryingly.

A couple of hours later…

"Where are we?" I asked them.

"Don't speak! You've got to stay quiet; no one is allowed to know about this," he angrily answered.

The car stopped. I looked out of the window; we were at the airport. We got out of the car. He turned to me and told me to get into a bag because they needed me to sneak on. So, I got in the bag. I had no idea where I was going; I had no food or water either. *What was going to happen to me? How was my life going to be?* I had no idea.

The Trails of Dread

by Leon Sharp

Chapter 1

I was walking in the woods; it was dead quiet. I tripped and fell into a bramble bush. I woke and found myself in a cave only with some familiar faces – they all turned and looked at me. I was very confused and still a bit tired. It was very dry for a cave. Everyone was still staring at me, waiting. I broke the silence.

"Why are you all looking at me?"

They replied with, "How did you get here?"

"I fell in a bush."

Silence fell over the cave. I looked around. There was no sign of any exit or entrance. I looked around.

"Hey Chris, you're on fire!"

Chris panicked and ran into a wall. I noticed a giant screen on the wall. It turned on. There was writing on it.

Chapter 2 – The Monsters in the Cave

It read, 'There are monsters in here so watch out, you need to find a way to escape him – you need to sacrifice something important to you.'

There were panicked mumbles, then there was an electrical shock. I turned and saw that John had electricity around him. There was a loud roar from a giant passageway, then a giant flower came into view. It looked like a decaying spider but a lot bigger.

It pounced on me - I screamed, but at this point Chris woke up and accidentally shot it with a fire ball. He looked shocked. Everybody stared in awe. I was being mauled by a giant spider. I punched it. It flew back.

How did I do that? I thought.

A fight broke out behind me. I stared in horror as the people got shocked and melted at the same time, when I noticed we were being suffocated by giant spiders.

We attacked first.

Chapter 3 – The Great Escape

Chris shot one, I punched one, and John and Harold attacked it with acid and electricity.

"We did it," I said, "We finally killed them!"

I noticed a box with a weighing device with a saw next to it.

Oh no, I thought.

We walked over to it.

"We have to cut off a limb," I said.

We shuffled around uncomfortably.

"I'll do it," I said.

"Are you sure, Ethan?" said Chris.

"I'm sure – you two have people you care about. I don't."

The pain was unbearable.

A wall collapsed, revealing a forest. We walked out. It was beautiful.

The Loop

by Archie

"Aaah!" I heard, as I stumbled down the ancient alleyway. The ear-piercing noise filled my brain with questions. *What was that? Where did it come from?* I stumbled down the alleyway – I could hear the sound getting closer and closer. Suddenly it went pitch black. Someone grabbed me. Their wet slimy fingers; I could feel the sharp edges of the scales.

BANG!...

There was a loud thud. The sharp, needle-like nails jabbed into me. I could hear whispering all around me. Suddenly, it all stopped. I couldn't hear my heartbeat or anything. I couldn't hear myself think. I was stuck there, just standing on the spot.

"WHO ARE YOU? WHERE ARE YOU?" I yelled.

No reply. I could smell dampness and mould. It was revolting. Under my feet was a slippery cobbled path. Suddenly I started feeling very tired.

THUD!

I dropped to the floor. I slowly closed my eyes. I was back in my room; questions filled my head. *What just happened?*

"Ben! Ben! Time for school."

I got up, slung back my duvet and ran down the creaky old stairs.

"Mum, mum, where are you?"

Quickly I ran downstairs and sprinted to the kitchen. Breakfast was already on the table. It was my favourite. Fresh orange juice and cornflakes. Until I realised something was wrong. It was the milk. It was cow's milk, which my mum knows I'm allergic to. As questions filled my head, there was a loud

BANG!

My heart was thumping in my chest. I started feeling dizzier and dizzier.

Thud!

I dropped to the floor. I slowly closed my eyes. I was back in my room; questions filled my head. *What just happened?*

"Ben! Ben! Time for school!"

I got up, slung back my duvet and ran down the creaky old stairs.

"Mum, mum, where are you?"

Quickly I ran down the stairs and sprinted to the kitchen searching for signs of my normal life. Phew, cornflakes and orange juice, mum. Until…I saw the door. The handle was wooden. After a long while, I decided to open the door. As I walked through, I could smell dampness and mould. I was back in the alleyway and there was an ear-piercing noise. I needed to break the nightmare. I needed to see who this was. I started walking around until I kicked something. It was a flashlight. Quickly I turned it on and realised no one was there. It was all in my head.

Saphron

by MacKenzie Lockhart

Chapter 1

Hello, my name is Saphron Thunburg. I am 14 years old. I am turning 15 years old next week. I am very short for my age. I have long, blondish, brown hair and I can be shy sometimes. I can't wait till my birthday because on my 14th birthday my boss told me that if I keep up my terrific work I may be allowed to become a starter chef.

If you didn't know, I have always wanted to become a starter chef, maybe even a famous one, because when I was younger my Auntie taught me how to make her famous spaghetti dish, but two years later I found out that my amazing Auntie was murdered for her money. Luckily they didn't get any money. You want to know how I know? Well, it's because I got all her money. Which was 10 billion pounds and 10p.

I already know how to make a lot of recipes such as chilli, homemade ravioli, pizza, homemade cheese sauce, and a delicious tomato soup. To be perfectly honest with you, being a chef is my dream job. But mostly, I want to cook for the poor. Did you know, I have a job as a waitress? I've been a waitress for almost two full years.

I was walking to the restaurant that I work at. As I reached it I saw hundreds of poor people. Yikes. I stepped in a dirty brown ice-cold puddle – my shoes were ruined. Oh well, I guess. Turning the corner, I was shocked. I froze, stuck to the floor. I knew why it was really busy there. It was because the restaurant had closed DOWN!

Chapter 2

Just as I saw the 'Closed Down' sign, a lady came up to me and said, "P-P-Please Miss, c-can I have some food?"

And at that moment, my eyes lit up in joy and happiness because I knew for a fact that my dream of cooking for the poor could come true. I bent down and said, "I don't have any food on me right now, but why don't you come home with me, and I will cook for you there? It will be nice and warm in my house and so will the food."

So, she agreed, and we went to my house.

When we got there I sat her down. I put on my apron, and I made my Auntie's special spaghetti Bolognese. This is how you make it – oil – onion – spaghetti – secret ingredient: a little bit of coconut – and I topped it off with my homemade tomato sauce. I gave her a portion and she loved it. She said, "T-Thank you s-s-so much f-for the delicious f-food. B-bye bye, dear."

The next day I was putting up my flyers advertising my cooking for the poor, and five people (that are poor) asked, "Can I have some f-f-food p-please?" and I said the same thing as yesterday and did the same thing.

* * *

This happens every day now; today I cooked for 705 people.

Chapter 3

Five years later, and today I have to cook for 1,000 people. I have already cooked for 950 – I just have fifty people left. Reaching the last person, this person is really cold, dirty, and mysteriously has a hood. Giving him a bowl of my spaghetti, he opens his mouth and fills it.

"Mmm," he says. "THIS SPAGHETTI DISH IS THE MOST WONDERFULEST thing I have ever eaten. You must come and work in my restaurant."

Then he took off his hood. Oh my, it's Gordon Ramsay.

"Wait, really?"

"Yes!!" he said.

Chapter 4

It's been five years working for Gordon Ramsay and I love it.

* * *

Thank you for reading my story. I really appreciate it.

Thank you.

Byee…

The question still remains is Saphron sweet like you think she is or is she evil and killed her Auntie for her money and the recipe and to be famous??!!

Girl in the Fog

by Elodie Oldbury

Dancing to fog, flowers brushed against my legs, my hair flowing to the wind. I felt the coldness on the tip of my nose. Paper-white daisies danced like ballerinas. I felt like I was floating then I opened my eyes. I saw a black shadow turning over me. I ran. I felt it coming for me. I could hardly breathe. I thought I lost it. But I kept running.

When I got home my mum was sat at the table writing. This was the first time I saw her up – not black-out drunk.

"Mum, what are you doing?" I asked, confused.

"Bills," she said, casually.

My eyes went wide. She never does bills. I just said, "Ok."

I ran upstairs; I decided to have a shower. I turned on the shower; the water trickled down my arms. As I massaged the shampoo into my long hair I thought, *what is it?*

I didn't open my eyes. I washed the product out of my hair. I got out, got dressed. I walked out, my hair dripping. I went to my

room and turned on the blow drier. The lights started to flicker
– I didn't mind it – then they lit, then went again. I tuned the drier
off. I tiptoed to the hallway and there it was – the shadow.
I quickly ran downstairs out of the door. I glanced at my mum,
teeth stained red; she dribbled on the paper. I slowly moved her
head on the pillow. I realised the shadow was still upstairs.
I quickly ran out of the door, slamming it shut. I got in the car
and drove as fast as I could not going over the speed limit – I
couldn't afford another ticket. I looked in the mirrors – I saw it
running after the car. I started to quicken it up, but the car started
to screech, then it stopped. I got out and looked the shadow in the
eyes.

It was my dad. I have to know why he is here.

The Sea Monster

by Josh Curie

Intro

The boat tipped and turned, and the monster attacked and dove into the deep never to be seen again!

One month earlier…

Chapter 1 – Prepare

"Have you heard of the monster?"

Ocean looked puzzled.

"What monster?"

"The sea monster!"

Ocean still looked puzzled.

"Have you not read the news?"

"No," Ocean said.

"Anyway, do you want to go fishing?"

"But you hate fishing," said Ocean, confused.

"But I thought I would try it," said Timmy with a smirk.

"OK, we will go prepare."

So, they prepared. Ocean brought scuba gear, a fishing rod, a spear, and a portable cooker. Timmy brought food, snacks, crisps, pringles, steak, fish 'n' chips, and some salt and then they set off. And this is where it all went wrong.

Chapter 2 – The Mistake

So, they turned on Ocean's boat and Timmy suggested the Bermuda Triangle, so Ocean turned right towards the Bermuda Triangle.

On the way they chatted about the monster, what it looked like, if it's protecting something, and Ocean caught Timmy chucking some raw meat overboard.

"What is that for?"

"It's for the sharks so they don't attack us," said Timmy.

"Suspicious," Ocean whispered.

Days and days passed, and Ocean was getting more suspicious of Timmy. But when the day came the last straw snapped.

Chapter 3 – Close to Death

Ocean realised Timmy's plan when he saw him taking a look at Ocean's fishing spear, and Ocean stopped the boat suddenly and walked towards Timmy and said, "You want to hunt the monster."

Timmy looked confused.

"H…how did you figure it out?"

Ocean was so mad: "You used me."

"I'm sorry," cried Timmy.

Ocean was so mad he punched Timmy overboard.

"Help, I can't swim!"

"YOU USED ME."

"I'm sorry."

The boat shook and the monster emerged from the deep, swallowing Timmy. The boat tipped and turned, and the monster attacked and dove into the ocean, never to be seen again!

A Story

by Jayden

I woke up in my bed. Outside I could hear the sound of an engine. I got up to look outside and looked out of my window, and there was a McLaren car sitting on my driveway. I quickly got my clothes on and sprinted down the stairs like Usain Bolt and opened the door. There he was, Lando Norris, at my doorstep. I could have screamed out loud with excitement but before I could he said, "Get in my car, I have a surprise for you."

Trying to calm myself down, I said, "Sure, why not?"

So, we - in slow motion - walked to the shining orange McLaren glistening in the sun. We drove off into the distance onto the motorway. We arrived at the McLaren F1 Factory; we parked in Lando's special car park spot at the entrance. We hopped out of the car and walked into the factory, and I was speechless. On both sides I could see trophies in glass cabinets. I could see one trophy saying 'Lewis HAMILTON' in big bold writing and on the other side said SENNA.

We carried on walking down the endless hallway with big wooden doors. First of all, he told me, "Come through here, I think you will like it."

We came through and there was the actual F1 racing car he drove. I was so excited, this time I screamed out loud. He shoved his helmet and put it in my hands and said, "Hey! Want to go into the simulator and have a drive?"

I said, with even more excitement, "Yes, I would love to."

We walked into a pitch-black room - as we walked in the biggest TV screen turned on. The bright light was blindingly bright.

Lando said, "Hop in the simulator, what track do you want?"

I said, "Austrian track, my favourite."

"Same", said Lando.

I started my lap and went through turn one, but then all the lights go out and it's even darker than before. I heard the smash of glass shattering and the alarm turn on – it was a deafening sound.

I woke up. I was in my bed and sat up. It wasn't real. And I said to myself, *it was so real.*

I could hear my dad shout at me, "Hurry up, you're going to be late for school!"

I got out of bed, and I felt a pain in my arm. I had a shard of glass stuck. I pulled it out.

DRE

AMS

Accident

by Honie Jeggery

I didn't mean to kill her. There I was hovering above her, on a hill so far away from home. My hands were shaking; I dropped the blood-stained shovel on the floor and glanced over at her. She had bruises scattered all over her body, her clothes drenched in blood. I had so many thoughts flooding over me. *Why did I do this? Did she deserve it? Where do I hide her?*

I didn't mean to do it, it just happened; *this wasn't my fault, right?* Her blood crept towards me, swallowing my shoes. The evidence was everywhere. I picked up her wrinkle-dented feet and lifted them into the black bag.

The blood stained my fingernails. My friends and I sat and glanced at each other. We were speechless, and I think we all had the same sick feeling in the bottom of our stomachs.

It all started when the new girl named Katie joined the school, her long blonde hair and her green shimmering eyes - she seemed so different. She always had her headphones in and jewellery covering her skin. Me and my friends thought it would be funny to play jokes on her; they were funny at first, but they soon turned dark.

The jokes started off with letters, deep letters. I would confess my feelings for her. I would tell her things about me; she didn't even know who I was, but I still felt disturbingly close to her. My obsession with her grew bigger. I think I crossed the line when I sent the chicken head to her door. I could tell I was getting to her – in school she looked fragile, hurt, shaken. I watched while she glanced round the hallway, trying to figure out who was doing this.

She saw me glancing at her in class – I was sat the opposite end of the room facing her. There was an empty seat next to me; she picked her books up and walked over to me. I loved her confidence; I could still see the fear in her eyes, but I think she just wanted to make friends. She pulled the seat out and sat next to me and began talking. We became closer and closer every day. She still didn't know I was the one sending the disturbing letters and gifts. My friends saw us hanging out and they began teasing me. I was scared of love, and I didn't want them treating me like that. I didn't want to be known as the person who fell in love with the new girl. I wanted people to see me as a cold-hearted mean girl. I hated the new me and I knew I had to do something about it.

I decided to meet her in a café for drinks. I had my hair in a low ponytail and I was wearing my favourite blue jeans. The café had small, circled tables with flowers and plants scattered. It had a cake stand and beautiful decorations on the windowsill. She arrived; her eyes sparkled as she entered. We sat and drank tea and talked about the upcoming tests at school. My phone buzzed in my pocket, and again, and again. I took it out of my pocket and scowled at the messages: 'You two are so cute'… 'We can see you guys through the window, how adorable are you both?' … 'You two dating?'

I was so annoyed; I hate when my friends tease me. We left the café and went for a walk along the fields, but the messages didn't stop. I couldn't concentrate, my head was spinning, maybe I didn't love her, maybe this was a mistake. I ran over to a big bulky tree and picked up a small, thick branch off the floor. She ran after me and tapped my shoulder, calling out my name. I turned. All my anger leaped out. Without thinking, I hit her with my branch. She fell to the floor, but I couldn't stop. My friends ran up to me; they were following me and saw everything.

Why did I do this?

Her Mind

by Felicity

Alice was your average loner. She always wore a typical stained grey hoodie with a broken zipper. Her hair was always in a messy ponytail with little wisps sticking out. Loud music constantly blasting from her old headphones. Her torn red Converse were the only things that made her remotely noticeable. If it weren't for her killer shoes she could be a nobody.

A couple of months ago she had this crush on this guy – Reid. She would stare at him across the courtyard, watching him laugh with his friends. His brunette hair looked soft and clean; Alice imagined it felt like the finest silk. His blue eyes were piercing with hints of hazel. Every so often his beautiful eyes would meet hers and he'd flash a smile, showing off his perfect, pearly teeth. But then it all went sideways. He started talking to all the wrong people, the groups that hated her. They twisted Reid's view; he now saw Alice the way everyone else did – a nobody.

A few years back Alice and her dad, Mark, moved to a small house in Chicago. They had to change schools and jobs, but it had been worth it for a fresh start. Before, their life in Brooklyn had been perfect. They had lived in an apartment with Alice's grandmother. It was a bit titchy, but they didn't mind, they were happy.

Everything had changed after grandma had died though. Mark couldn't afford the flat by himself with no help from the retirement cheques. The bills started piling up.

Finally, the debts and the worrying had become enough; Mark decided they needed a change. He had been looking for jobs in Chicago for just under a month when he found the most perfect one. It paid very well – enough to buy a house in Chicago and still have money left. He then sent his resumé and was hired four days later. This was the change they needed – but it did nothing.

Ever since her grandma died, Alice had been more alone than ever. She had no friends to talk to, and she obviously wasn't going to casually chat to her father, so she was left alone, trapped in Chicago with her music and her red Converse.

Alice's favourite pastime was writing in her English class. There was an unspoken freedom – anything you wanted could be painted to a page, to create any picture, to capture any image, to grow any idea. Alice always felt as if writing was an escape from her prison: her mind, the prison with no escape.

A week later, Alice walked into History and saw a new seating plan projected onto the board – *oh my*, she thought to herself, *I'm sat next to Reid.*

For the past months, Reid had been hanging out with his new gang nonstop, causing him to pick up their snooty behaviour. His nose stood upturned, unwilling to acquaint itself with anything but the sky. He was now too good for Alice and Alice not good enough for him.

"Hi Alex," Reid said, flashing a smile; it was once kind and well-mannered, but now it's nothing more than a coy snarl.

"It's Alice," she snapped back, glaring with cold eyes.

"Okay class," Mrs Johnson said, "I can see you guys have noticed your new seating plan and I'm glad to say this person will be your partner for the project."

There were groans from the whole class.

"Sorry to ruin your weekends," she smiled.

The bell rang.

"Where and when are we doing the project?" Reid asked, picking up his bag. "Library after school?"

"If you're not too busy with your cool friends." Alice rolled her eyes. "What am I saying, of course you are."

Reid smiled. "I'll be there."

It was five past four – he was late. She was on her phone texting her dad: 'Might be home late – looks like I'm doing the project alone.' She pressed send with a sigh. Then she heard the library doors creak open.

"I'm here!" Reid shouted walking around the bookshelves. He had a black eye, and his lip was bleeding.

"What happened?" asked Alice, with a worried tone.

"Just a little fight, nothing to worry about."

He smiled, a genuine smile. This time, Alice smiled back.

They were an hour into the project when Reid said something he had no right to.

"Shame your red shoes don't suit you, they're the only things that make you stick out."

Alice closed her laptop and started walking off.

"Where are you going?" he said, raising an eyebrow.

Alice put down her laptop and picked up a marble statue. She imagined the blood strewn across the blue carpet. The gash in the side of his head. The horrific screams from everyone else in the room. But then, she thought better of it. Alice put down the statue and picked her stuff back up.

"Home."

She was now alone again. With her grey hoodie and broken zipper. The red Converse – her only friend. She was, once again, a nobody.

The Commander*

by Joe Thurtle

I don't even have a goal anymore, how can I? When all that surrounds me is death and suffering; this war has taken my family, my ambition and my dignity. Everything in my body is telling me this needs to end.

"Commander," the driver screams in a terrified voice, waking me from my gaze.

"Commander, we…"

"We what?" I exclaim.

"We are low on fuel," he mumbles.

He's only a kid, I think to myself, *his whole life ahead of him.*

"What should I do sir?"

"I don't know, Kurtz."

All our outside fuel had been lit earlier by a defector traitor. I don't understand how people can side with those 'liberators' – they're liars! When I was just a child in the Great War, some soldiers came and beat my dad then burnt him alive. Those so-called liberators are lower than human – they are animals.

"Commander!" his screams echo through the tank, bouncing off the thick steel walls.

"I…," I exclaim.

"What, commander?"

The gunner introduces himself. He is 23 and has been serving with me since '42, it's late '44 now. November, in fact.

"Sir," the loader shouts.

"All of you calm down."

"Don't."

"On that treeline then for Chrisssakes," I demand.

The track treeline itself gives us some good concealment but still not enough, as slowly the engine erupts into life. Deep grey smoke rushes to escape through the exhaust. The damp and dark mud clenches in between the treads as it is propelled forward.

"Sir," the gunner exclaims, "Shall we prepare?"

"Good idea," I state, sarcastically.

All of us simultaneously jump to station and hop out of the tanks. We are still one short as of late: not enough people for just a bough gunner. Our driver can do that job – hopefully – I mean, we're stationary. As it's autumn there are more than a few dead plants to use as makeshift camouflage.

"Kurtz," I demand. "Grab that foliage."

"Why sir, what's this going to do – delay our deaths by two minutes?

"Kur_!"

"No! It's pointless, they're not coming back."

"Don't…" I interrupt, "We will retreat through the bridge then," I say in a crazed state.

"We don't have a bridge; they've already blown it. They lied. There's no reinforcements, no retreat, no safety," he shouts.

"I, I – just do it already," I yell.

His skin-tight pale hands rub against the sandpaper-like bark; he violently chucks the foliage on the front plate shield of the tank.

"Commander!"

The loader screams, slightly breaking his tone.

"Look."

He hands me the old beaten-down binoculars and points them in the right direction. It's smoke from an engine, a convoy heading this way.

"To the tank," I scream.

"What is it, Sir?" Kurtz asks.

"Americans."

It's 10:37pm now; the lights are slowly wandering this way.

10:48pm – still nothing here quite yet, but it's dark now so we have the element of surprise now.

10:54pm – The grease trickles down the turret ring as it steadily rotates into position. It clicks into place, a huge armour penetrating 88mm round is loading; making a slight ringing noise that echoes round the tank, finally settling down.

"Fire," I scream.

A deafening ring bleeds out, echoing through the Tiger. The shell breaks through the muzzle, leaving an enormous shockwave and a trail of black smoke. The shell impacts on the hull of a M4A2 Sherman, striking its ammunition rack, igniting all of it. The American crew desperately tries to escape as the luminous neon fire slowly burns them alive. A shot from the convoy strikes the Tiger's infamous armour and bounces straight off. The loader picks up the golden brass shell and slams it into the breach.

"Fire," I yell.

Another Sherman erupts.

"Fire."

And another.

"Fire."

Our ears are bleeding as the final round of ammunition is released upon their souls.

"Use anything you can," we howl.

I pick up an old rusty MP40 machine pistol and chamber a round and prepare for our final minutes.

And here we are. We die, faceless.

Just four people out of millions to die, just statistics.

Dreams

~~~~~~

Shorter pieces
from journals

My Dream to Become a Muddy Puddle
by Harry

Ever since I was two years old I've wanted to become a muddy puddle. Mummy always says, "Peppa, everyone knows that's only a myth!"

Despite that, I've never stopped believing. One day, I will become a muddy puddle!

I always look outside and it's raining.

"Can I be a muddle puddle?" I ask to Daddy.

"No, it's not possible."

"I'll find the instructions to become a muddy puddle."

"The instructions don't exist."

Despite that, I've never stopped believing. One day, instead, I will become a dinosaur!

I always walk into the museum with George, and I look inside the dinosaur room.

"Dinosaur, rurr," George would say.

With one word, I became a muddy dinosaur! My dreams came true, I became a muddy puddle and a dinosaur!

And I regret that wish every day!

By Honie

I have really strict parents; they have such high hopes for me and expect so much. Truth is, I'm not very good at maths and English and science. Baking is what I enjoy and it's my dream to have my own café.

I haven't told my parents this; I even lie about my grades.

I dream about having a small cosy café, my own kitchen I can decorate and be free. I would have a couple of tables and a cake stand. I would make rich creamy hot chocolates and coffees and tea. I would have apple trees at the back of the shop, with some benches people could sit and eat at, a small pond, and plants scattered.

I'm hiding a big secret from my parents. I have a sick feeling in my stomach. I try to tell them, but I'm scared they will be disappointed. Truth is, I got into a cooking college. It's a big white building with loads of cookery rooms and lessons every day. My friends are also going; it would be so much fun.

By Katie

My Dream is to create my own version of Alice in Wonderland. I would start by nobody having any worries and everyone would be friends. Young, energetic children running around. Sweets and money hanging off the trees. Everything would be perfect. A wonderful, sparkling waterfall where baby deer come to drink from, but when you put your hands in it they're dry.

By Logan

The thing stopping me from living my dream of manufacturing cyborg glow-in-the-dark things like PCs or penguins, is the school I attend. They don't believe in me, and they won't let me take days off to study my creations. My parents believe I can do it, so I won't let anyone hold me from following my dreams.

By Callum

Every night I have a dream, a dream of ideas for inventions. One night I was dreaming about a way to stop climate change when a faint moan and a gurgle drifted to my ears. I jumped up and a big black cat was staring at me. Every night this keeps happening right before I get an idea. Stupid Big Black Cat.

The Phoenix Dream
by Josh

A long time ago there was a phoenix with a dream to help and change the world. Its tears could heal a wound in seconds. One day the phoenix saw a wounded snake and used its tears to save that snake's life, and then the snake saved a mouse, and the mouse saved an ant, and the phoenix saw that a little thing goes a long way.

By Elodie

Baking, it's my favourite thing to do. I love to bake; it calms me, and it makes me happy. I want to start my own café with cakes and macaroons, scones, teas, coffees and all types of food. I want my café to be cosy and homely with fake plants – cuz I can't keep anything alive – I want sage green touches and cream highlights. I want it to be a hangout.

I finally Got my Dream Job Only to Discover That...
by Archie

"Yes Yes Yes!!" I shouted, as I finally got into Yeovil Town's academy. I couldn't wait to go to training. I was so excited, and a bit nervous. As I pulled up, I could see all the players doing warm-ups and stretches. As I jogged over the hot-headed manager ran over and started shouting at me.

I had no idea what I did wrong. "What are you doing?" he yelled.

THE
BANK
OF
DREAMS

&

NIGHT
MARES

I have a dream

The Beaminster School project allowed pupils from Years 7-9 to immerse themselves in the creative writing process over a period of six-weeks to produce the 'I Have a Dream' anthology.

Our purpose was to provide the young writers with the toolkit to write freely, with the outcome of a published book. The writing process is messy and non-linear, and each young writer had a journal to explore that process, unhindered by thoughts of marking, grading, or assessment.

We started with discussions about ideas, where they come from, and how to harness them, with insight from Neil Gaiman about how a confluence of two seemingly unrelated thoughts can create something entirely unique. From there we gradually assembled that writer's toolkit, with sessions on dialogue and character, point of view and structure, and story-planning, with games and tasks to allow that creativity to emerge.

The pupils were uniquely placed to explore their ideas with volunteer Writing Mentors assigned to small groups; without the support of Amberley Carter, Charlie Goldsmith, Nick Goldsmith,

Alex Green, and Eleanor James, the anthology would not be what it is.

The Bank of Dreams & Nightmares' ethos is to offer child-led creative writing workshops, to listen to young people, and learn from them. By offering small group mentoring as we did at Beaminster School, the children are given time and space; what they have to say and write is nothing short of remarkable.

The fallout from Covid-19 is an ongoing challenge in education, and children have endured an exceptionally tough time. There is much talk of 'gaps' and 'catch-up', and we must remember that for some children it has been a tremendous struggle. The Bank of Dreams & Nightmares exists and strives to offer a safe and creative space for those young people to be heard.

It's a credit to Beaminster School to recognise the power and impact this kind of enrichment can have; special mention goes to Naomi Gribler for co-ordinating the entire project with us, with thanks to headteacher Keith Hales for having us. Also big thanks to Helen Pinkett in the library, who offered such a warm welcome each week, as well as tea and coffee!

We are immensely proud of the Beaminster writers, and 'I Have a Dream,' is testament to their engagement and the creative spark that is unique to young minds.

Jan Lane
Creative Learning Manager
The Bank of Dreams & Nightmare

About The Bank of Dreams & Nightmares

Our mission statement

Everyone's full of stories. Don't believe me? Well then off to bed and see for yourself. For when you sleep, the stories in your head wake up. Your dreams and nightmares come alive and start to play in a world of infinite possibility and never-ending imagination. And then you wake up. And reality brings them crashing to an end, cruelly concluding all that could have been. Well we're here to put an end to that, or at least a beginning. 1000s and 1000s of beginnings. Hear ye hear ye! We at the Bank of Dreams & Nightmares want your stories. Bring them in, in all their absurd, weird and wonderful starts, middles or ends. And we'll keep your story alive, keep it going, bringing it out of your head and into the cold but illuminating light of day. And we won't stop there. Oh no. Every story deposited in the Bank of Dreams & Nightmares gets interest. Like any good bank we'll help your instalment grow and grow. We'll give it eyes and ears to see and hear it, words to appreciate it and applause to motivate it on. So, believe in what's in your head, believe in what you can create, believe in your dreams and nightmares.

Our aim

get more kids writing and show them just how far their words can take them.

By

making them realise their weird, wonderful, absurd, ridiculous ideas are all story-worthy

Promising

that if they deposit them in our bank we'll bring them to life and help them accrue interest (i.e. eyes and ears to see and hear them)

The Inspiration

Valencia 826 in San Francisco

What we do

We are a registered charity in West Dorset and we offer FREE creative writing workshops to children aged 7-18 in the West Dorset area of the UK. We want to show children just how far their words and stories can take them, so we work with industry professionals to create inspirational workshops that all have a real world outcome. How about writing a campaign for a cause you feel strongly about and then seeing it made by professionals so you can present it to local government or businesses? What if you wrote some song lyrics, and then are able to see a real musical artist take your words and make it into a real recording you can share with the world? Or how about you become the lead defence lawyer for a special mock trial in a real court house where your persuasive arguments determine whether someone is guilty or not guilty? The possibilities are endless and at The Bank of Dreams & Nightmares we want to have fun showing children that it all starts with an idea, a story, some words, and where that can take you is the exciting part.

Our focus is on those children who are most under resourced, who normally do not have access to these types of things but deserve them just as much as anyone else.

We will be housed in a real bank in Bridport, but instead of money we deal in the currency of stories, and at the back of the store, if you know where to look, is a secret door that leads to the writing centre where the real magic happens.

We work with both primary and secondary schools during term time providing one-off story writing workshops with the end result being published authors or broadcast podcasts! We also work in collaboration with secondary schools to develop longer term long projects where the outcome is a published anthology of the young writers' stories.

We offer after school clubs for children to develop their writing and get involved in longer workshop projects that currently range from creating their own quarterly newspaper to a sketch comedy workshop, with the final sketches being made by professional actors.

The Bank of Dreams & Nightmares is committed to practically addressing educational inequalities and the opportunity gap faced by young people from less advantaged backgrounds. We work in communities with high levels of socio-economic inequality, where we are providing a critical link between local schools, arts organisations, higher education institutions, and the commercial sector.

Our aim is to help children and young people to discover and harness the power of their own imaginations and creative writing skills. The Bank of Dreams & Nightmares strives to improve children's behaviour, engagement, essential life skills, and wellbeing – the root causes of exclusion.

At its core The Bank of Dreams & Nightmares is also about something much broader and more inclusive; it is about using the creative practice of writing and storytelling to strengthen local children and teenagers from all backgrounds, to be resilient, creative and successful shapers of their own lives.

Impact

Through our programmes, young writers will have felt listened to and have had their opinions valued and acted upon. We can demonstrate the impact creative writing has on young people. We provoke and empower them to think creatively and help them to unlock their imaginations. Then we publish their writing, providing purpose and value. The impact will demonstrate significant shifts in motivation, attitude and behaviours - which in turn affects health, ambition and resilience.

Our Workshops

Primary School Storymaking workshop

In this two and a half hour workshop we work with a class collectively to create a story, whilst one of our volunteer illustrators brings the story to life as it happens. The first half of the session has the class of young writers voting and creating as a group as one of our volunteers scribes the story for them. Once they get to the cliffhanger moment each writer then creates their own ending to the story, with the help of our story mentors. After the session we take the words and pictures and make them into a beautiful bound book with each participant getting their own author biog at the back and space to finish their individual ending. It is always a fun and lively session, and the results have been wonderful.

Secondary School Pod casting workshop

In this one-off workshop we work with a class of young writers to develop a personal essay about identity. The workshop normally lasts around four hours as we explore different aspects of the self and what it means to our writers. It is always a lively and interactive session and the final outcome is to record each essay as a podcast, which is broadcast via our soundcloud page.

Secondary School
Six Week Story Anthology

In this longer programme we work with one group of students to develop an anthology based on a chosen theme. We work closely with the school to decide on a theme which complements the curriculum for the chosen year group. At the end of the six weeks we make the final anthology into a published book, one of which you are reading now. All the proceeds from the sales of the book go directly back into the charity.

The Vault Newspaper

This is our after school workshop that takes place every Thursday of term time. Here we work with a group of young writers between 10 and 15 years of age to create a quarterly subscription based newspaper. In the issue we look back at the news from the last three months and the writers share their perspectives on the news stories that they have selected.

We have many more workshops being developed, and will hopefully be able to share them with you all very soon.

People

Founder
Nick Goldsmith

Creative learning manager
Janis Lane

Volunteer Coordinator
Alex Green

Board of Directors
Mick Smith
Simon Deverell
Joel Collins
Niki McCretton
Simon Hawkins

Our Volunteers

There is absolutely no way any of this would be possible without our incredible volunteers. These incredible people work in all realms from story mentoring to illustrating and beyond. They range in age, background and expertise but all have a shared passion for our work with young people. We salute you!